Phyllis Hartley

Artist
Sculptor
Writer
Found Art Collector

Editor: Mary Kane

Photography: Mary Kane, Jim Morgan, and Eric H. Edwards

Design and layout: Jim Morgan

ONE BIRD BOOKS

AVAILABLE AT AMAZON.COM AND BARNESANDNOBLE.COM

Door by Mary Kane
The Ant and the Map by Judith Benét Richardson
Harlequin's Guitar: A Fable in 67 Improvisations by Jim Morgan
Little Hours: A Novel by Lil Copan
Procession of Souls by JimMorgan
Black Apple: Collected Prose Poems by Eric H. Edwards
Luminous by Mary Kane and Mark Bilokur
Crows by Jim Morgan
In the Book I'm Reading by Mary Kane
Quaker Minims by Eric H. Edwards
122 Days by Angela Rose and Mary Kane
Jazz Midnight by Jack Crimmins

ISBN: 979-8-9898147-2-5

One Bird Books
35 Brush Hill Road
Hatchville, MA 02536
www.onebirdbooks.com
onebirdbooks@gmail.com

Phyllis Hartley

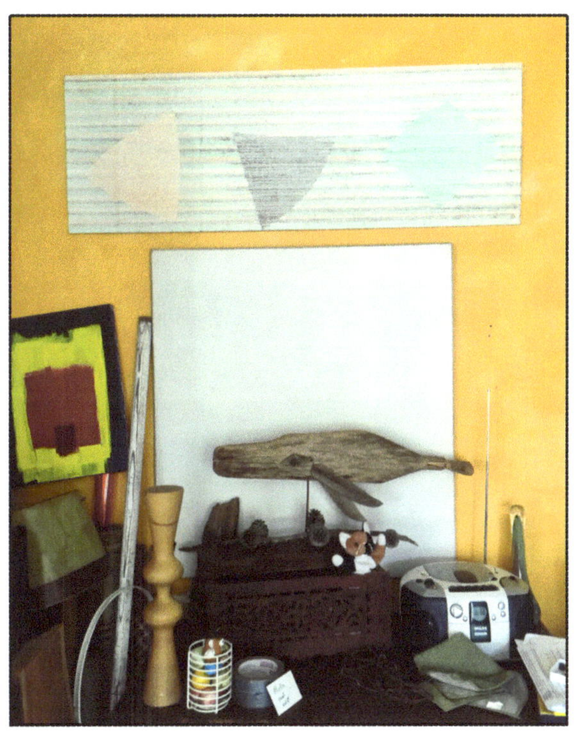

Artist
Sculptor
Writer
Found Art Collector

Introduction by Eric H. Edwards

One Bird Books • Falmouth, Mass.

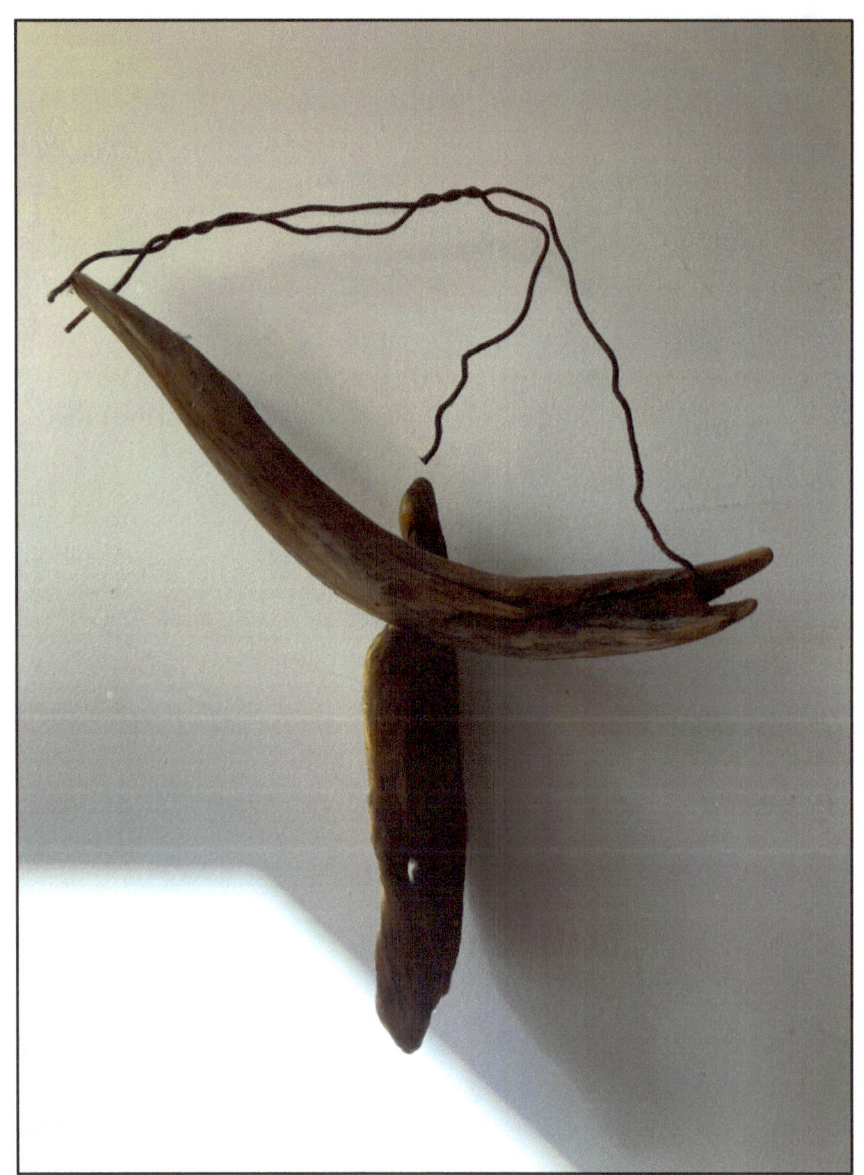

CONTENTS

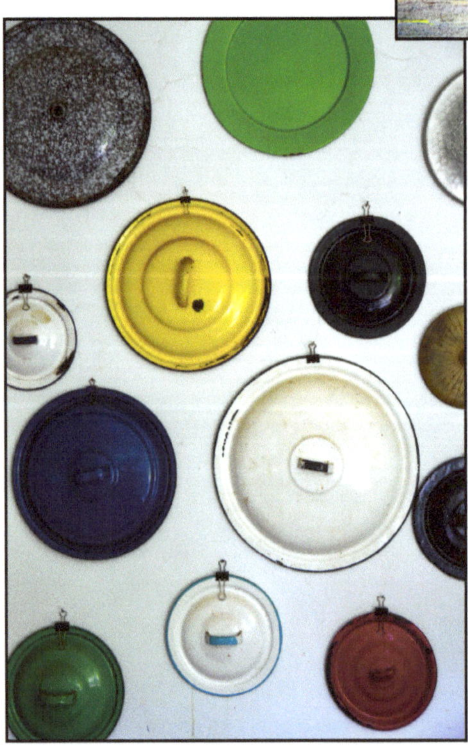

By Eric H. Edwards

"Obtainium." Her word.

Phyllis was trained, she was technically proficient, she mastered any media she turned her attention to, and she worked well with others. She was also often a loner. Though if someone gave her an idea she would run with it like a lioness, seeing what it might have within it before, well, understanding its implications often better than the person who gave it to her. Those implications would become works of art alongside her own. Phyllis was intellectual. She lived an artist's emotional life, out on a windy ledge that made it difficult, sometimes, to hang in with her.

Obtainium. One piece of her production.

She would take literally any object and use it or just keep it around because it was full of potential that she hadn't made out .... yet. Phyllis didn't hoard, but the stuff in her yard was overwhelming. She would tell me as we walked around, talking about this piece of metal or wood, that she really needed a warehouse, not so much for the neighbor's sake but so she could wander around with her stuff laid out for easy examination. So she could see it and think about it without distraction. She never had that kind of money.

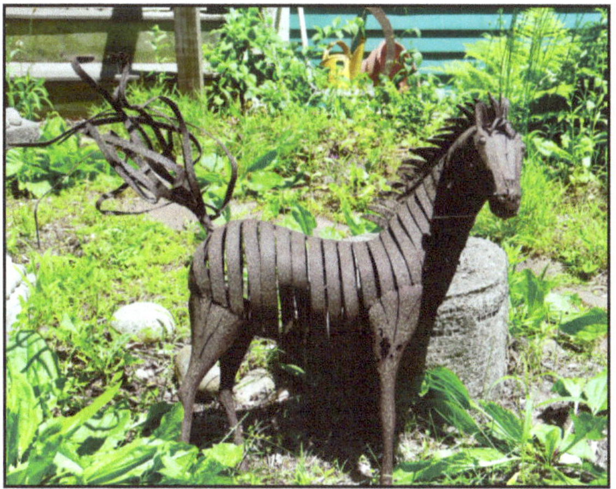

On her front porch steps was a series of stones she picked out of the beach to make a chess set, sort of. Or maybe it was for a game like chess, but with other characters; other not-just-men, undefined rules and moves, and what sort of board would that need?

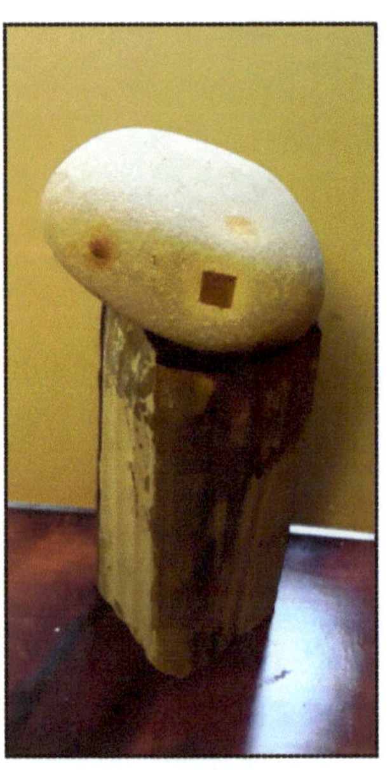

Another one of her pieces consists of a short, square (obviously vintage or antique) section of gutter drain pipe on end, with a stone jammed into it that was undecorated except for one thing, the square worn crystal on its smooth, ocean-polished surface. Or perhaps the large furniture was more accessible if unaffordable, a series of pieces that belonged in a museum at once, like some surreal impracticality of domestic life, or in some wealthy estate's hallway beneath a painting by her of the letter "e," font helvetica bold. San serif please, keep it plain but monumental.

Obtainium. Good for theater sets, too.

When Edward Gorey wished for a piece of almost-furniture for one of his Cape Cod productions, Phyllis was happy to oblige. She set other plays as well. She could be gregarious when she worked on a project with others. She was wholly engaged. She seemed to meet everyone with the same intensity and enthusiasm. If you were paying attention, she was, too. Perhaps she thought of her sets as art objects that actors moved around in, an environment not at odds with the nature of the play, but enhancing, part of the audience's enjoyment for that evening.

Obtainium. Any expertise could be acquired.

Words were a constant food, the life of art and social existence, the intelligence and freedom of ideas.
Poetry offered the same interrogation of her interior life that objects did. Words just get managed a little differently. Or found a home in the midst of paint, carpentry, wood burning.

Obtainium. Her word.

Phyllis even found/made the word that suited her work. An element not readily obvious in nature, not easily placed on that table of specific measurements, but the element that illuminates the world where something thought of sometimes as trash comes into contact with human inspiration. And by that painful and ecstatic alchemy becomes herself, a work of human art.

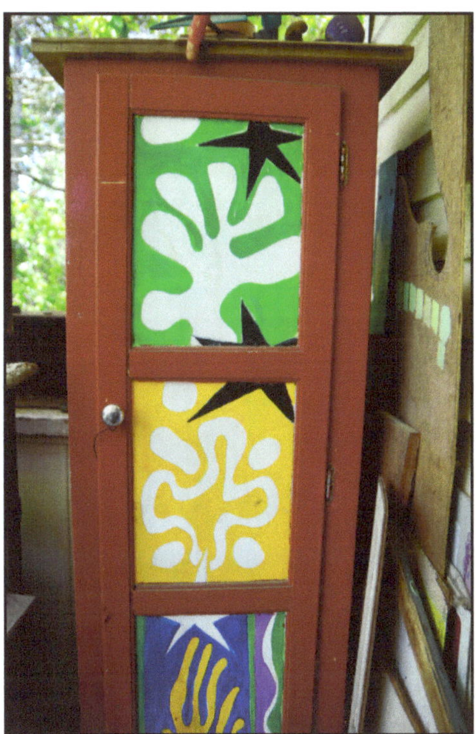

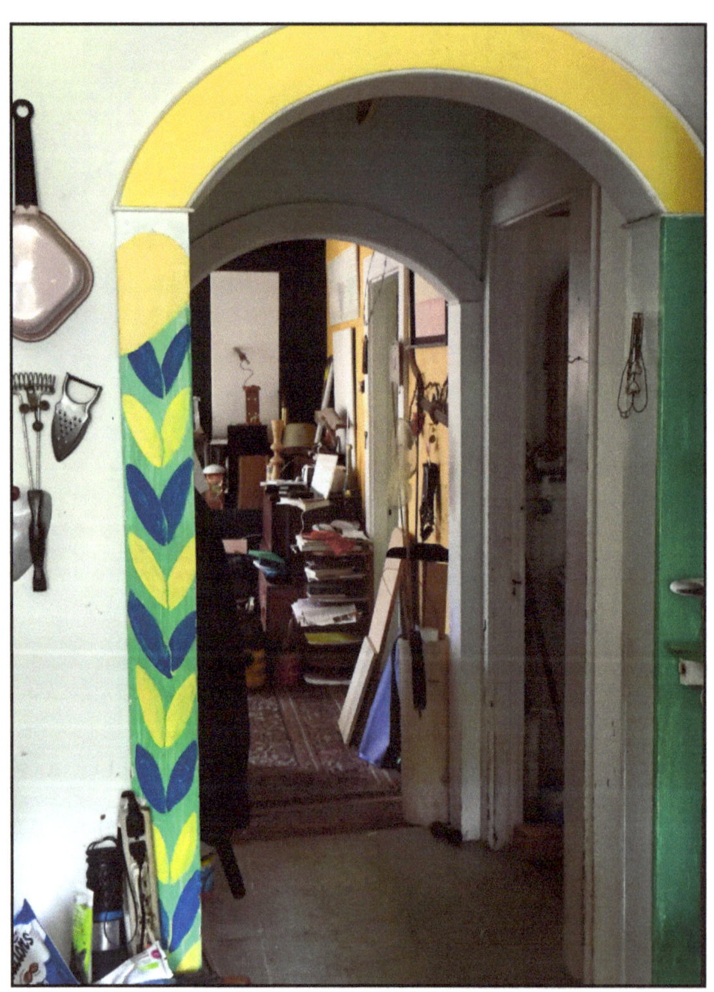

x

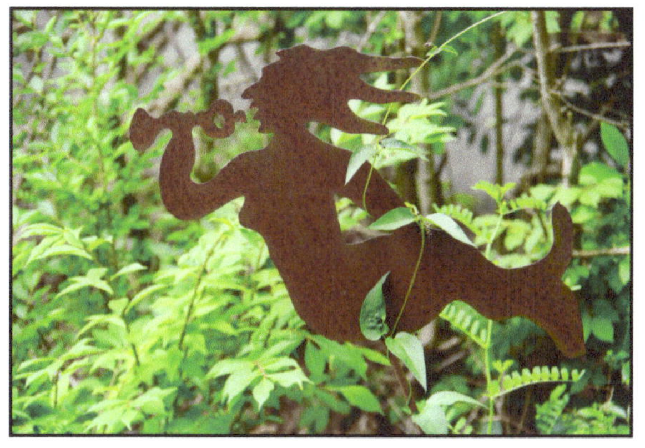

I have not told you about the grass and its greenness. Look at that word "greenness." It really does deserve all those esses, the swoop and curve back. Yes, and I have not told you about the white and tan sand that you can dig with your heels and toes. I have not told you of the wind that flaps the brim of my hat up and down when held at just the right angle. Otherwise it's just down or up. And the reedy noise it makes, the funny old battered and bent thing, that I reshape the brim every day I wear it. Or this I have not told you, but I have seen. A rainbow. It's a specialty of the light in the sky and the water in the air. And how it hovers in the air dim and bright, dissolving slowly more and more difficult to see. I have not told you to find and hang onto these things, things outside of you but given mind space and deep concentration, holding it for real in your mind and mind's eye. Concentrate on just that one thing. The bands of color, the smell of the sky, the order of the tree line. Concentrate on I am here right here feet in the sand, the coarse sand with footprints over footprints that in six hours will be gone leaving water to crash over it. I'm sorry I have not told you. It was important for you to know and practice. To know and practice for when the void visits. Then you could use all the things I have not told you and tell them to me.

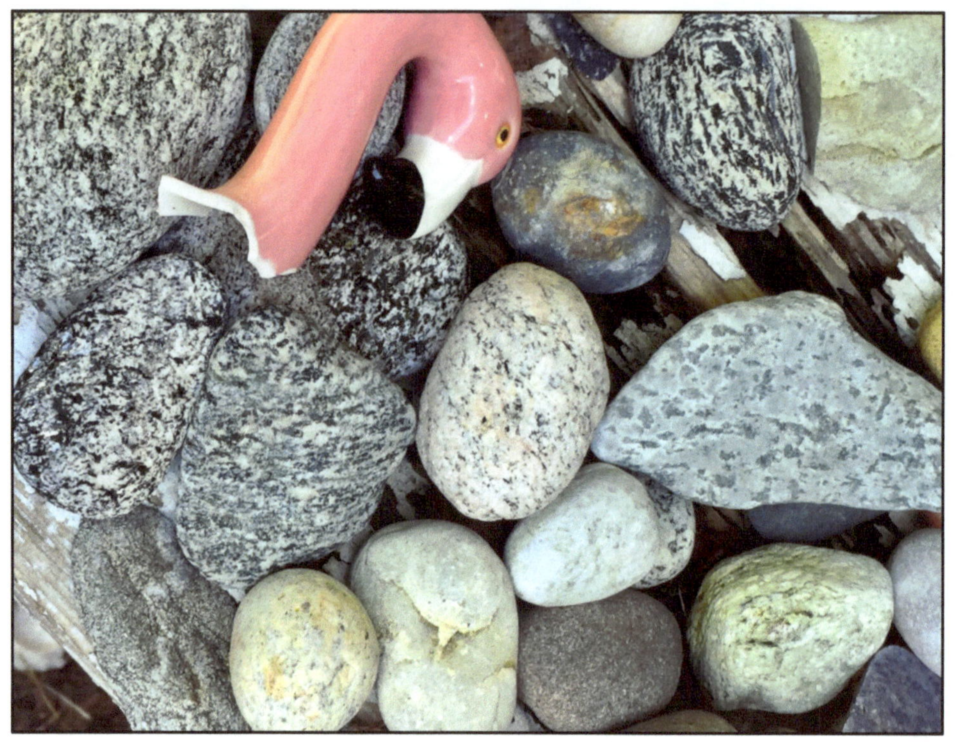

ODE OH DEAR ODE DEAR

An ode to an egg. The shape
Just the shape.
Searching and searching
Beach after beach
For the perfect egg stone
The failure brought home
For final inspection
Gut rejection and

Plop in a big bowl of almost egg

Eggs that fail

But still earn a place of discovery

So sit in a pile in a cement bowl

All colors

All sizes

All brightness

But where is the whitest of white

The almost an egg quartz in color

Rolled and roiled

In the sea

Beside me

But always failing to round out the last side

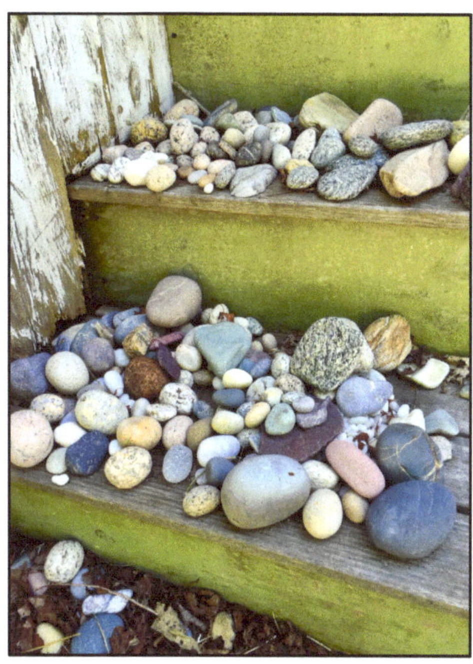

Which remains stubbornly flat
And fools me every time I get excited
There it is, perfect and also white
Now there are many colors of white
Which you will see
When you cast them out of the
Pockets, tins, bags, ____
And pore through them
All the white become gray white
Yellow white, cloudy white,
Clearish white
On and on
It's a double whammy to find an egg that's the right
Shape and color.
Your neck gets kinked looking down at the beach sand
And only half listening to the roar of the water
The rounded the stone as far as an almost egg
But no further. You chastise the sand for
Clinging to the stone rather than roll it and finish
the last bit to eggdom.
The collection grows
Its all I do now I'm retired
I look for the perfect egg.
I have to go to a physical therapist
To work on my neck so it won't be
Perfectly bent for egg hunting

And not for talking to people

Who start squatting down and tilting their heads on their necks

To be able to talk to me face to face.

Who needs that kind of behavior

When really you are perfectly fine and fit for your job

Of almost an egg roller of almost egg rocks.

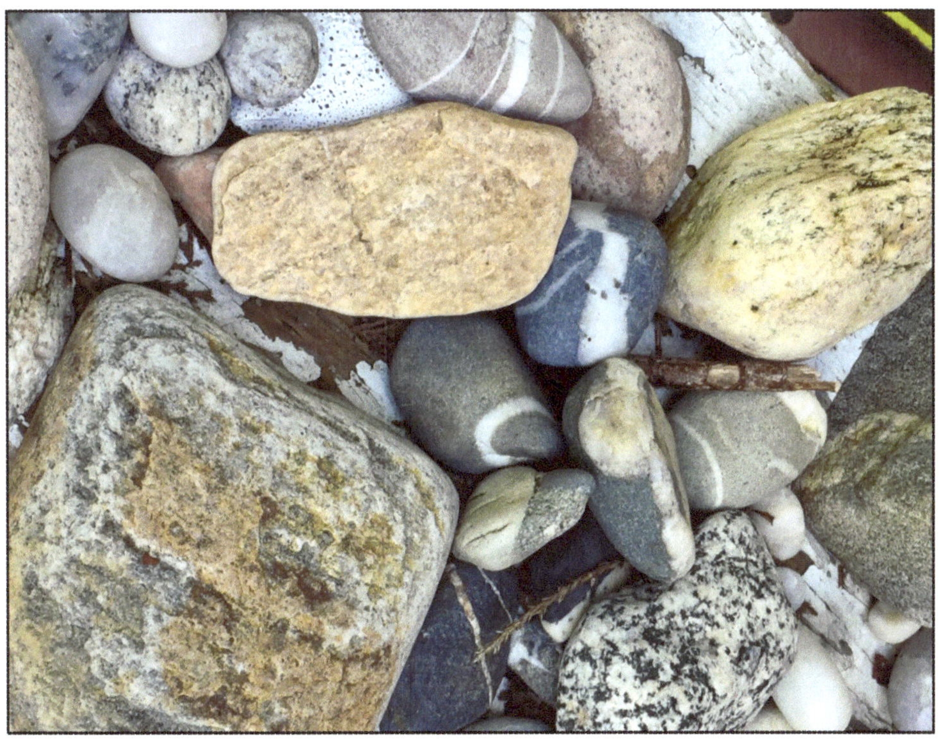

Everything that ever happened to me
is etched like a tattoo but not in ink,
real blood, not ink pen but cutting letters
with a knife tattoos. All hidden. My back

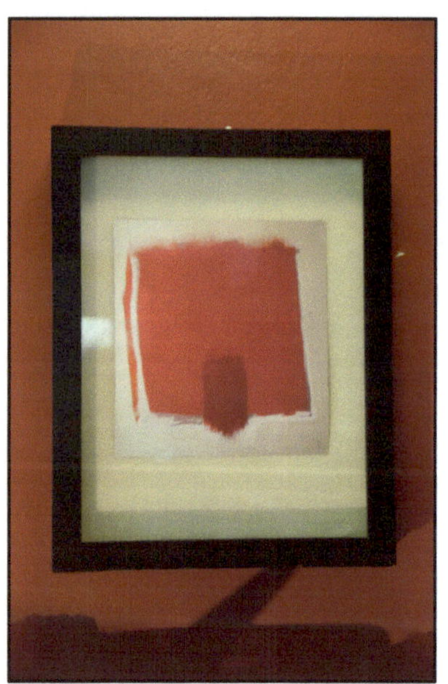

is a 13-page book carved slowly after what happened
happened. Who's to say it is an accurate telling,
no one ever sees me naked, but I stand before a
large mirror and read it all through. Aha, you say,
it will be all backward as well as hidden. Not so.

I always have the read mirror with me in my compact.
If I could, I would have a reduction mirror too so I could
read words in the smaller reflection. But the
carver of words has gone. I can't bear to carve them myself,
I am not that strong against the pain. I only ink them on
with indelible ink in secret places. Well, well, you say,
perhaps you don't own those memories, only
the carver does and is using you,
page after page of skin, for his own history, not yours,
think of that. I did, suddenly I did. After many showers
the indelible faded and became unreadable but the carved
words did not. They stretched and got misshapen over
time and I still kept covered those crimes
his not mine and their weight and depth reduced my
memories to strange dreams misty and unfathomable,
lying in the deep of my words and deeds.

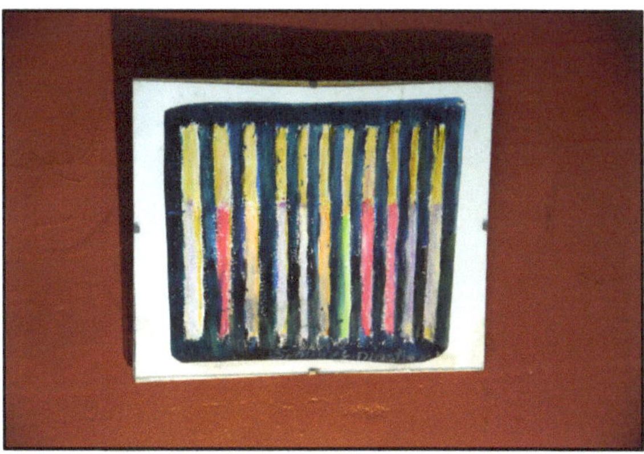

I decide on a piece of fruit. I make sure it can stand
alone on its own.
This is key to success.
Then I make the mold, careful to put a crooked
nail in its hole so it will remain
in the place for a stem
then wait hope and pray the cement will dry properly
and the mold will release without problems.
How many times have I bought the perfect fruit
only to find it days later soft, too spoiled
even to eat.
How many ways was I jerked away from
the forming of the fruit.
How many days went by I did not touch the fruit.
I'd make a damned poor fruit tree not minding my leaves
sap and veins to create the final perfect
result. A beautiful "living pear."
The workdays are spoiled like the real pear.
I must go to the fruit section once again
and pick the perfect standing one
and a couple of funky ones leaning lopsided
this way and that with a wonderful fat
stem to finish it off.

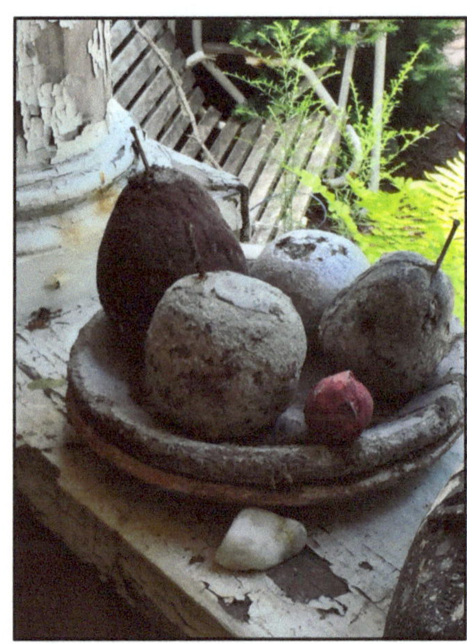

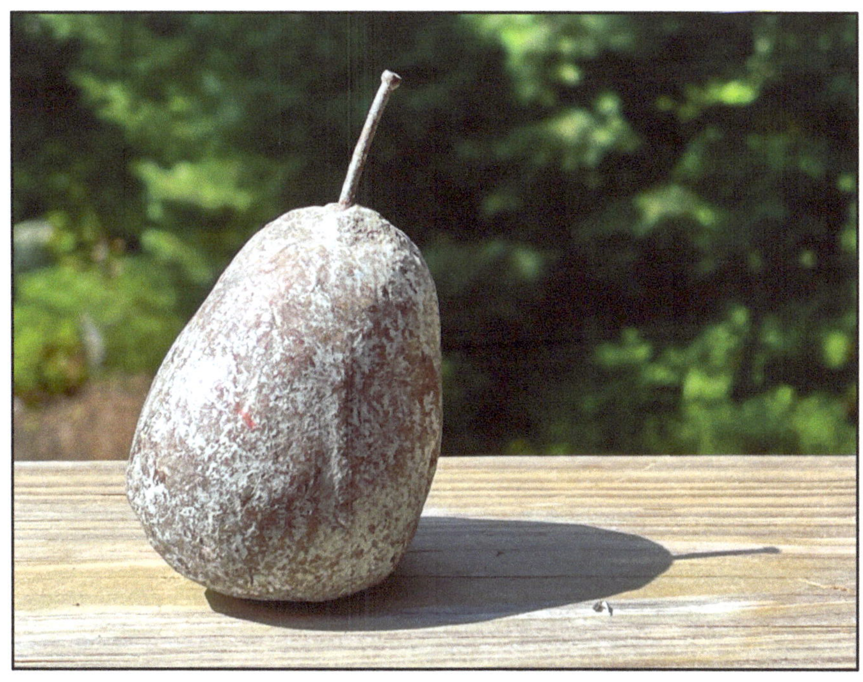

Now I am not behind it. Not behind the work.
Its time has passed, like old shoes lining the closet,
dusty and forgotten taking up space with negativity.
The past truly is the past
where skills unused are forgotten
where what once seemed natural
to work on or with is no longer in
the work vocabulary. Yesterday's news
yesterday's invention.

Plants festoon and need a lot of water
& snipping to become sculpture in
your home, she said, as we toured her loft of divisions.
Divisions of living, working, painting, sleeping
but damned if I saw the cooking division.

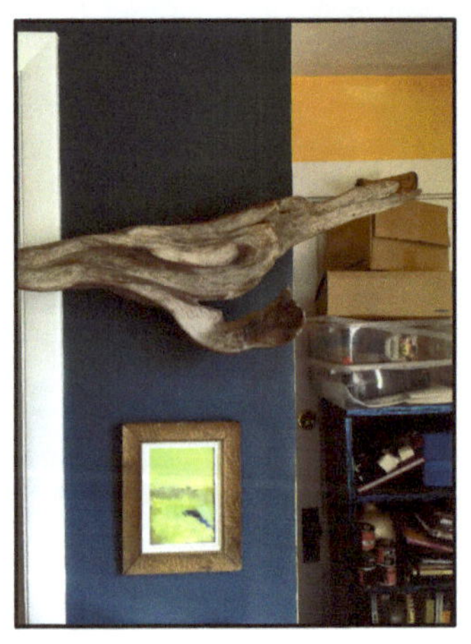

Some couches work, some just are.
Some tables work, some just are,
and this home decorator was a real control freak.
When interviewed by the photographer she consistently
turned the question around in a different way and
spoke with a certain authority.
Her home on the other hand did not portray
that force or chill. Warm colors, "sculpted" plants,
busy bright rugs lots of slants &
shoots. I wonder where she shows her paintings
and what they are. Is this the one who gets tired
of things and throws them out when done and fits
in new things even if she rearranges everything.
That's what she did with the interviewer's words.
Does she do this with her friends, her dealers
& strangers as well. What control of people & environment
she has. Kinda pleasant too. For me at least. Too
much impression of turning your thoughts around or

even writing them off with a word or 2 and substituting
her own question to answer or lecture.

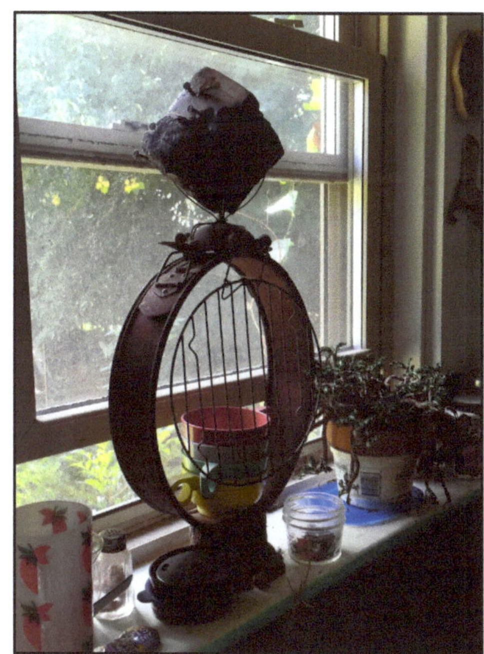

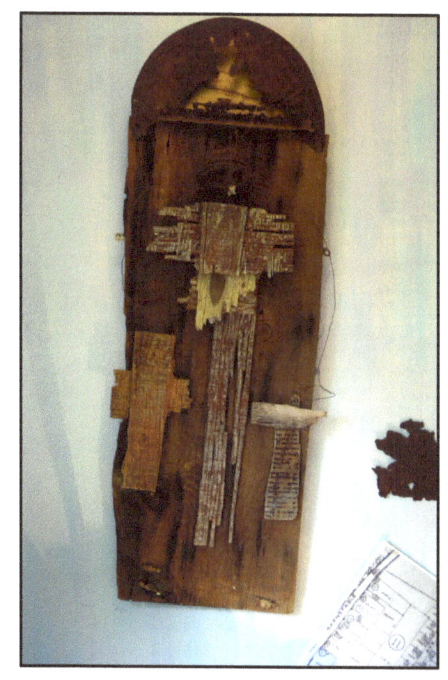

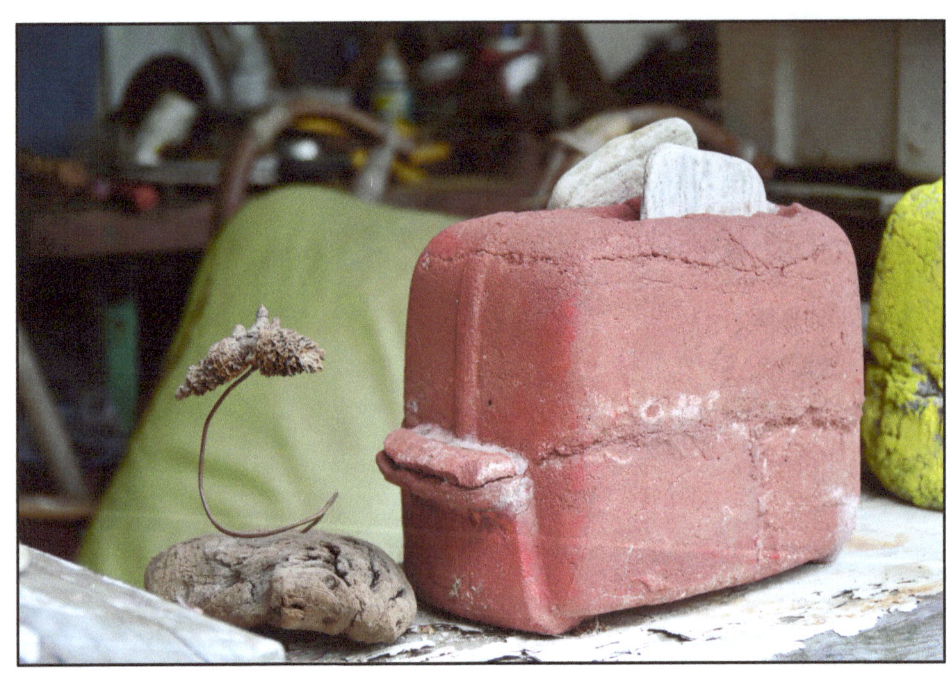

The music of my youth got me tapping & rock & roll dancing all around the kitchen one night. Years after my youth is it the physical memories in my body that grabbed onto the familiar beat or is it that the music is universal in some way & reaches across decades. I remember now the time I couldn't dance even though I wanted to. It was at my friend's 50th birthday party and I

wanted to work the
my friend Jacek could do.
the beat. I looked at my
move. Not so. Six months
after the dance I dance at
"Thanks God." I don't
"Thank God" dancing
prescription to take up.
room to room, scare the
down the walk which is
But dance down it I would
mailbox where the dog
scare the mail man who

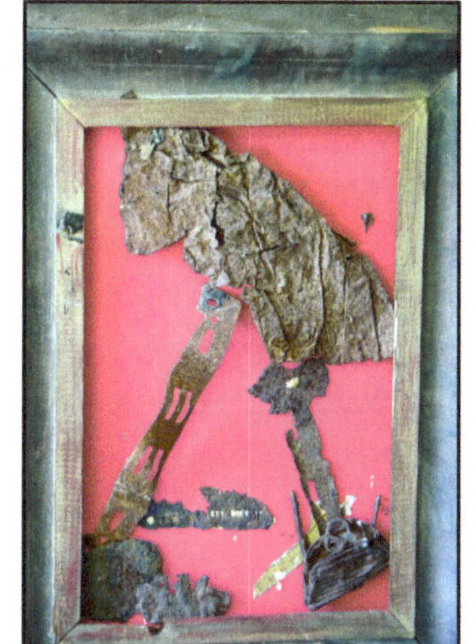

rhythm up and down my body like
But I couldn't even lift my feet to
feet and said, Okay, now you will
later I was diagnosed. Six months
my friend's son's bar mitzvah.
know how long I will last but
probably would be a good
Dancing across the house from
cats, and dance out the front door
uneven and a terror now to use.
and should. Dance around the
reaches the end of her rope to
instead of running away would

give her head and neck an affectionate ruffle before he left. I could wave a rock & roll goodbye as he delivered more good or bad or trivial news to be recycled and sent to China who now buys all the recycled paper they can get to wash and return to your phonebook and sketch pad.

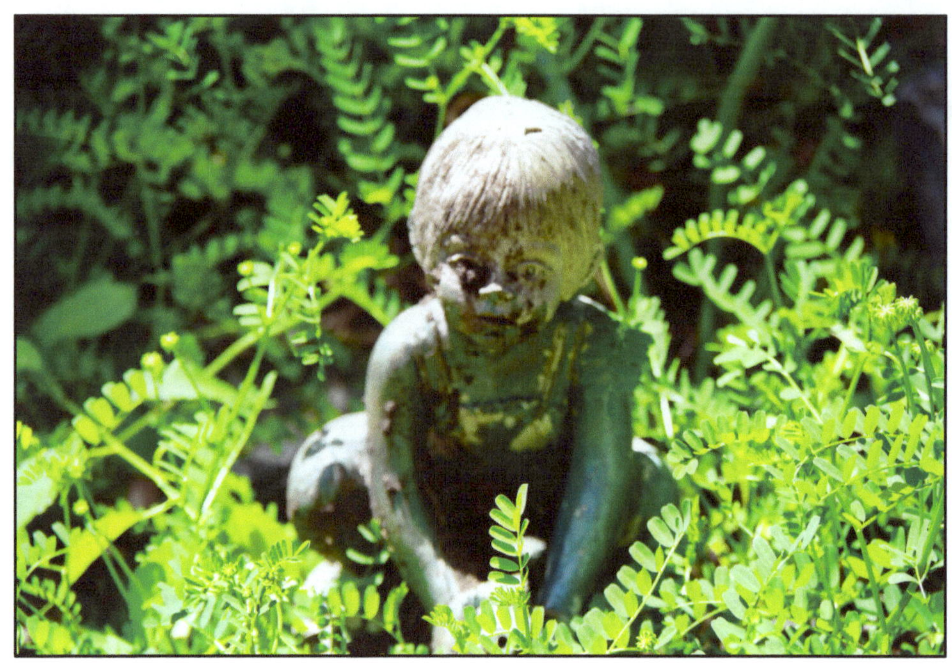

UNTITLED

You like to pretend you will see her again some day in Knoxville. But since you've never been to Knoxville it will be too bad. Much much too bad. Knoxville Kentucky was where my dad was stationed during WW II, "the just war" "the good war" or whatever they call it now. I'm sure back then it was a horrible war as all wars are. So will dad see her again in Knoxville. No probably not so much since he has a wife here and she's got a tight rein even though I doubt my dad would ever wander any further than the neighbor's house to stand with the kids while they wait for the school bus. But this music from Knoxville is dad's generation of music. Jazzy, big band, crooners, love songs, peppy instrumentals with the trumpet, trombone, and Benny Goodman's boozy woozy instrument. Now all that describes a time & hasn't made a comeback

14

in Knoxville. But it should. One thing about R & R of my generation it keeps coming back. The Beatles are popular again with preteens and John Lennon would have been 70 this year I think. Wonder what he would be doing now? Forsaken music for mystics for cynics or gone beyond cynicism to Ghandi.

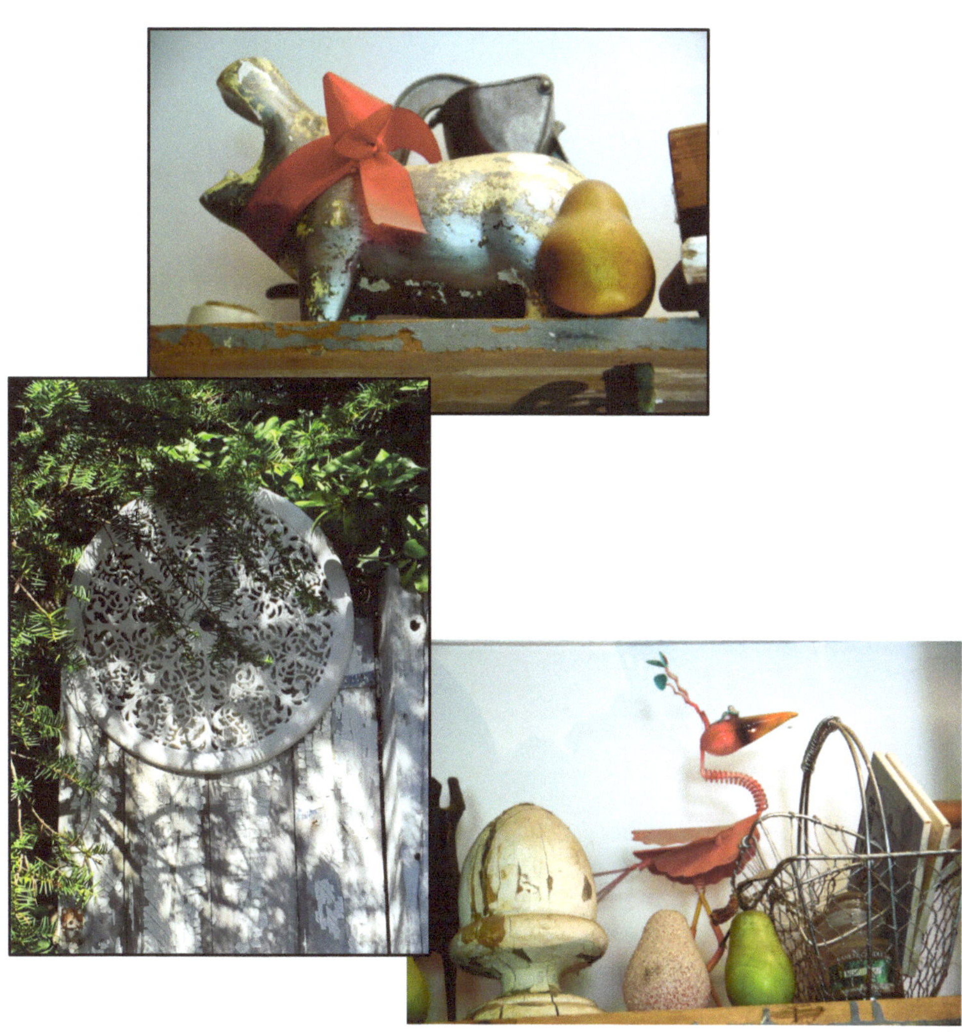

OBSESSIONS

I have an obsession about ice cream
But I don't buy it or eat it or write about it
Sometimes it bursts out on a hot summer day
And there I am standing in line listening
To the chit chat of 10 or 20 obsessed people
My kind of crowd.
But then
It ends
No more, my pants're too tight.
I had an obsession about sunflower seeds
I was putting them in everything – cereal,
yogurt, anything I was cooking.
I'd mix them with raisins and sneak
snacks of them late at night -
Protein – and boy do I need it.
Lately, because the price, comparatively,
was so low I bought 4 jars of
strawberry rhubarb jam
Delicious!
I wasted it on everything.
There's a new bakery in town
French
Boy do they know how to do bread

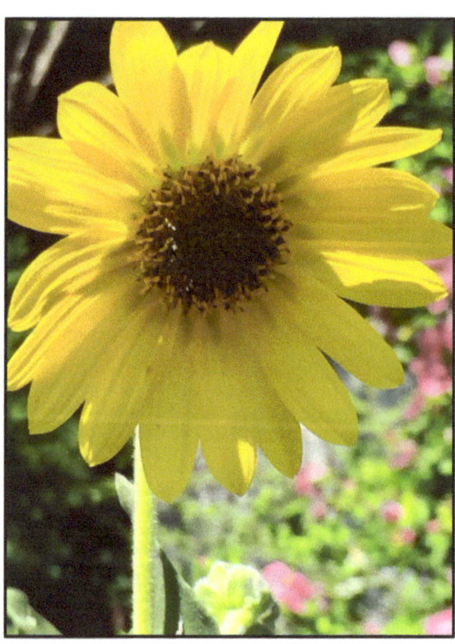

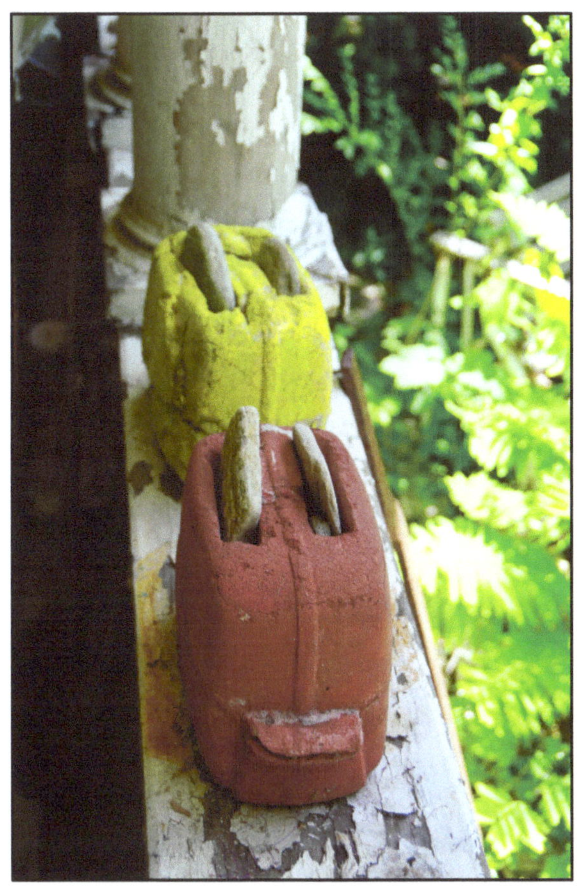

I'm part Polish with an uncle
Who owned a bakery.
Boy what bread
Its terrible to be prejudiced
As all know
But living in the Cape Verdean community
Makes me long for some hardy bread.
The Verdeans don't do it – at all
So now because of a new French bakery
On Main Street (so sophisticated seeming –
what are they doing in Falmouth?)
I am addicted to bread – of all things
I haven't eaten bread in years
Now I eat it with butter as a treat between
meals
How strange this is.
I have to go downtown (or should I say down
village – does
That work) to get my ½ loaf of chewy hard-
crusted bread.
You get the crustiness by spraying water into the brick
Oven during a certain part of the baking process.
But looking around this huge space that used to be just a shop
I see no brick oven only funny stainless-steel things.

I needed to open the refrigerator

But my hands of course were full

Is that always the way

But in addition to that

I had overstepped the limited lean space I have left

And was into the fall zone

The pitch forward balance knowledge gone zone

So I have to consciously wobble back

To straightened without dropping the handfuls

And find the straight zone

sometimes if I grab the refrig door

I can pull myself in or in reverse

If I push away from the fridge

I can stop myself from falling into it.

Sometimes I worry I will grab the handle

For balance

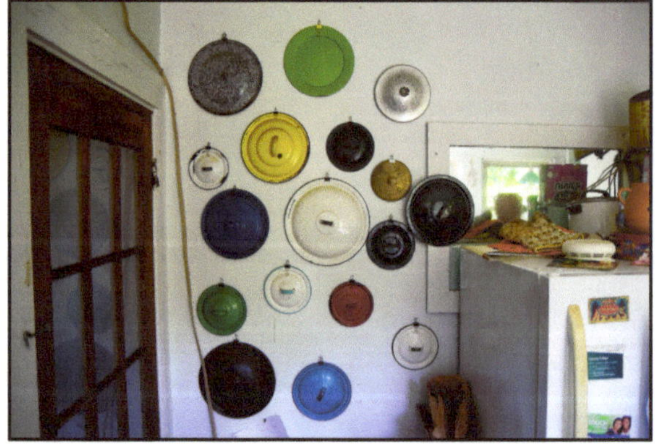

And it will be too much too far away and

The door will swing open because of my pull back weight

And it will pull the refrigerator on top of me

And there I'll be for days

Waiting for someone to find me

Or simply be unconscious and then not breathing

Lungs smushed

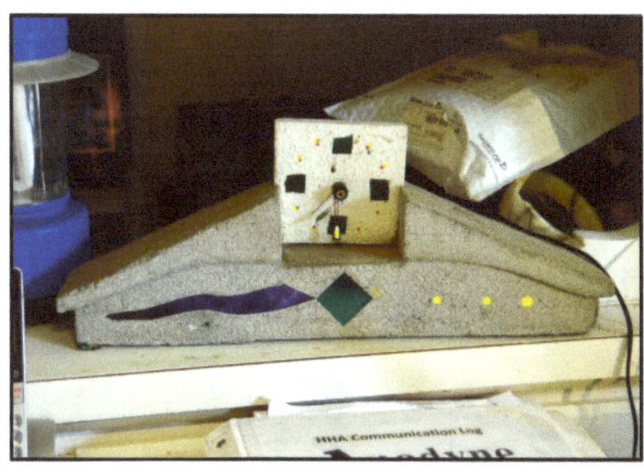

This is when I think of the tag my mother and
My aunt, both 93-years-old, wear that alerts someone
With a phone clipped to their ear
That calls up and asks what's wrong
But this only happens if you push a button
You have to be able to push a button
Or else you lie there all night
Like my mother did one night
And my sister found her in the morning
My mother claims she pushed the button
But it didn't work
But her arthritis is so bad she is capable of only
A little pressure
I don't have arthritis (yet).

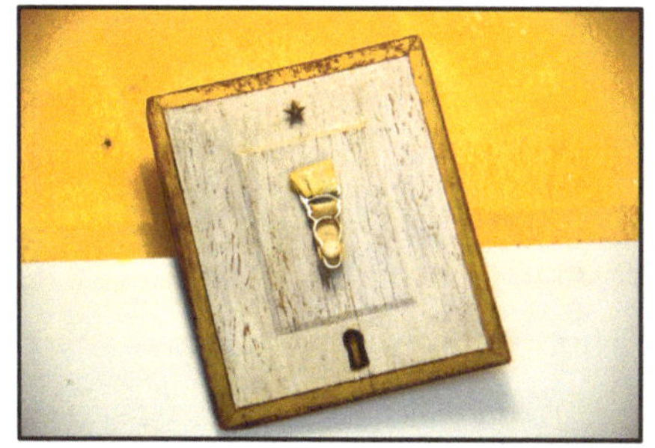

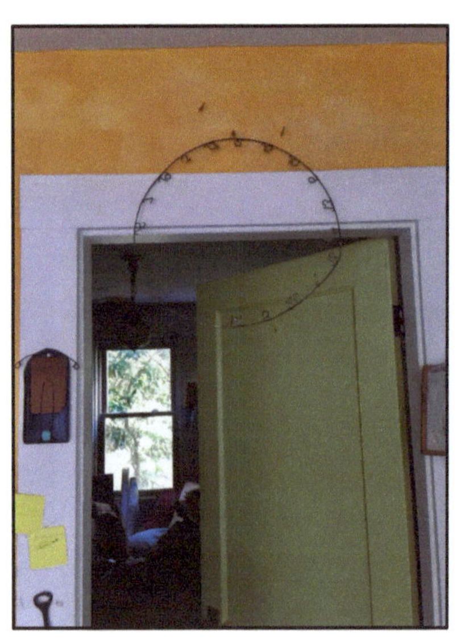

thrown on a table

a line comes

not of fishline or a clothesline

but, no these are not as much

fun, but a line is a line and one

must follow or be left behind

or so the postal service says in its

book of instruction with the blue

gray cover. So follow the line of the letter

back out the door to the once again empty

white box by the roadside

and follow the road like you never have before

look at every tree and blade of grass

look at the curious line of the bee

working the center of big floppy azalea blooms

it must be nice that finally there is

the means to make honey again. But off it goes

taking its line with it to impossible places to follow

look at the line of the road and the line

between every stone in the dirt road all curling

and connected for miles and miles into the foothills

of round top mountains where there is

a trail from the northern most state to

the south up and down the rounded mountains you climb
alone on your own line journey you sleep under trees
and look for huts left behind by line followers before you
for the crudest of shelters from rain and hail
falling down in lines above and around you
bouncing off your rain-soaked hat and the shoulders
of your jacket. There are fine lines that when
they reach you are diverted and bounce off
in all directions or simply fade away with too
much wet weight to move on
and they seep through your clothes and impress upon your
skin their power to discomfort you
now you wish for the lines of the sun's rays
to bless you with the strength of heat to soak up
your liquid mantle and once again make you
dry and warm

Wholly Bread

wholly bread
holely bread
holy bread

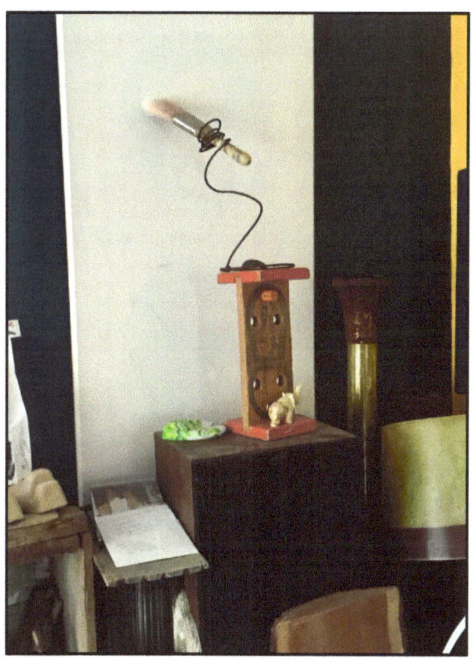

To be a writer and write things

Is a lot of fun if you just be silly

Said the man with the big red clown nose

I thought what a fine way to start a class

However as the class continued

Session after session the clown nose stayed on

And the clown suit progressed. First a clownish shirt

Then baggy striped pants then an amazing horn with

A big rubber bulbous making very loud sounds

Then came clown action somersaults, trips, marching

Crawling. It became so intense I decided to drop

Writing class altogether but said the official at the

Window of class selection you will lose all your

Money because add and drop is way over $1000 out of

Your pocket gone, But I protested he's a clown the

Professor is a clown in a clown suit. You know, I said

Mr Add and Drop. You kids keep telling me this. It's over. It's old

The joke is in the dead joke box. Deliver me from

Any more of this clowning around. Come to the class.

Come see this nutter teach, surely you would have him

Fired for this. I've been to your class all semester being pestered

By all of the students playing this joke and the class was orderly

And fine. There was no clown that time. I'm not going to

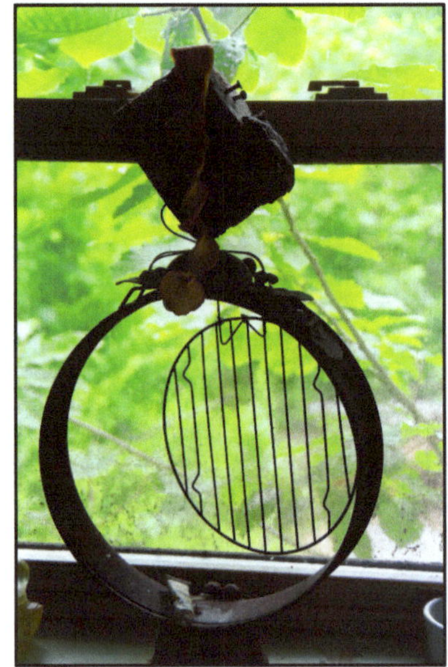

Monitor it again. End of issue and he slid the door

Of the add and drop and didn't answer my protesting knock

I could not lose the $1000 to a clown I will go to class and make it the

highlight of the day. And I went and I got up and started

Juggling the class went wild and many of them insisted

I teach them to juggle and I did.

I didn't pass the writing course

But received a complete rather than incomplete

I saved $1000 for my next career choice, sculpture.

In that class we memorized and recited poems by John Ashbery

I passed with flying haikus.

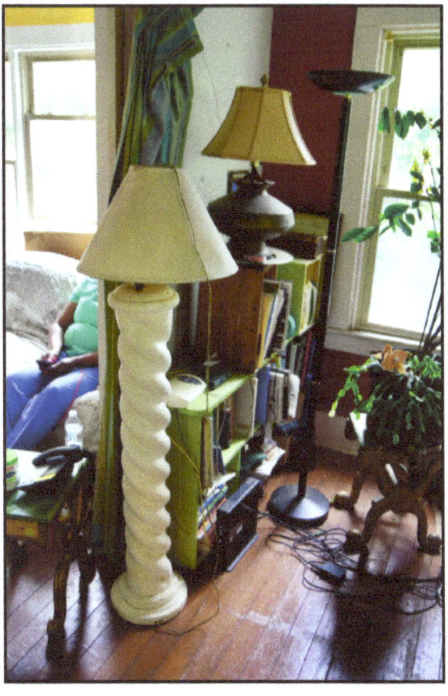

Smudged chalk dust on board and hands.

Stars start their motors powered by the wind.

Sinewy, is that a word or form of agony?

Perhaps just a twisted sinewy soul or maybe the sinewy

wind will find out the truth of this earth

and search for another truth somewhere in the stars

when the wind stops the blow. Truth dried out by

the sun is truth with capitals, light on in the computer keyboard,

and we know when the red light is on the CAPITALS dance

free, find a space and settle down in the universe because

they learned that there is no wind in the

universe just stars that dance the same dance but

different because it is a different moment in the cosmos

which only moves forward not back, not up nor down,

but you can burn your way home and visit the

neighbors who are curious about you.

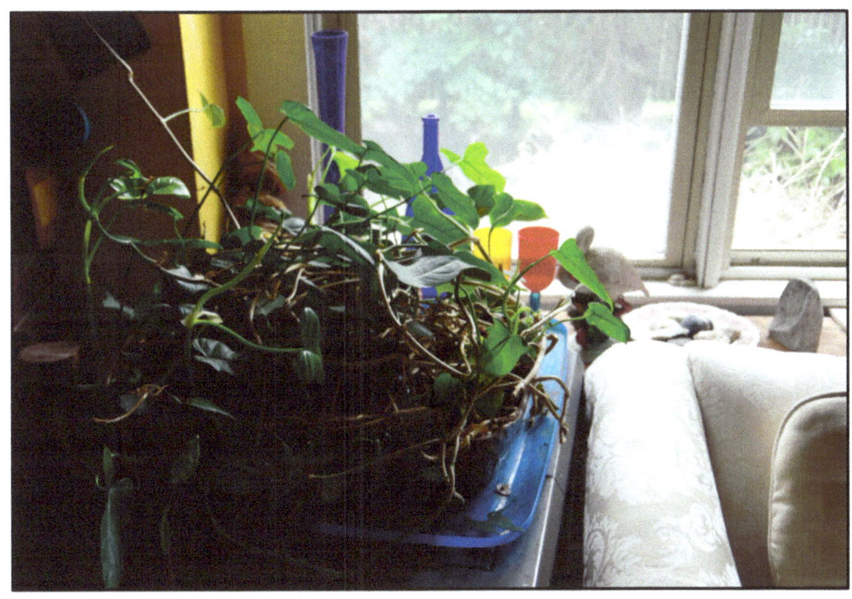

from Infrequent Poets (2000)

Amaryllis Twins

The amaryllis twins
Nod their luminous heads
Two violent shades
Orange and red.

Tongues unfurled
Brassy bold
With feet stuck in clay
Cold.

Rain
A wrinkle down the window
A wet promise glassed away.
A cat's paw
Dares to stray
Scoring the firm
Towering stem.
Green juice oozes
From parted vein
Gathers at score's end
Forms a drop.
Glistens.

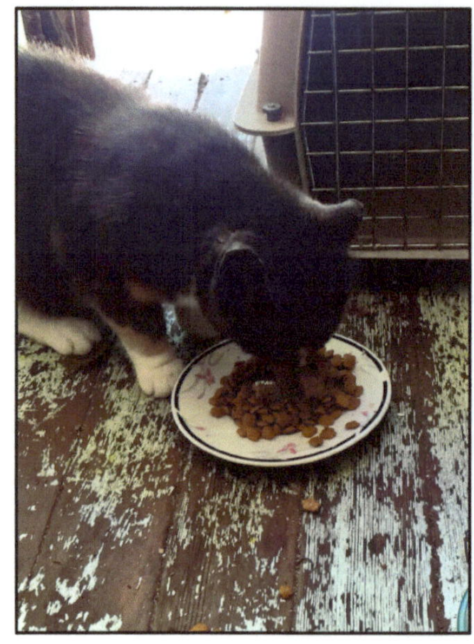

Touching the liquid to
Her sleep filled eye
A lover nests where
Pleasure wrestled and wrapped
Her limbs
And finally
Left her at rest.

She plots her work day
And never will suspect
There
On the back of her head
A sex hair display.

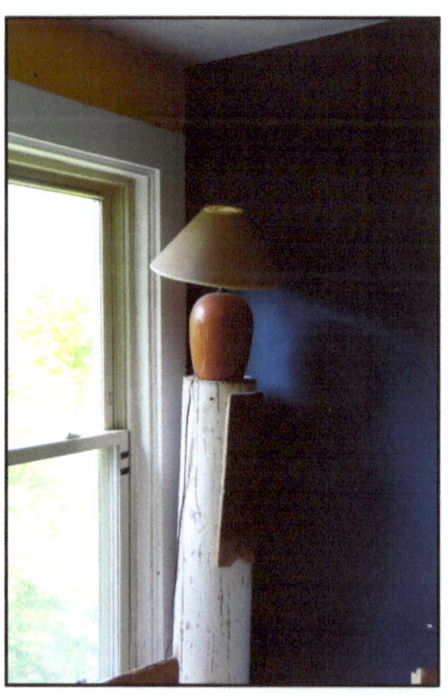

26

Knotted
Between her night and day
Boundaries crossed.

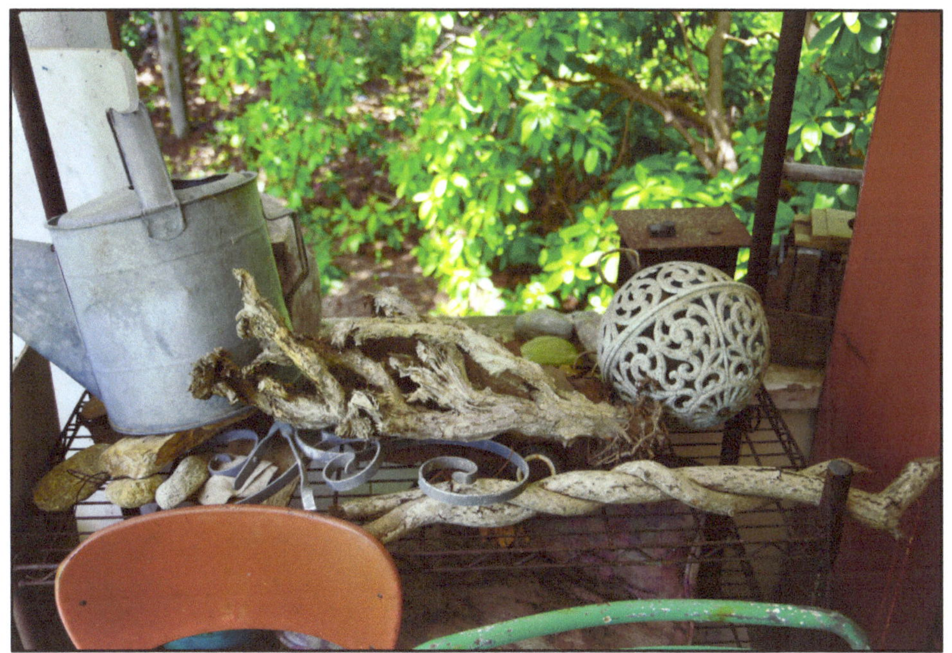

My lover dove back
Into her life
No longer coming up
For frequent kisses of air.

Fortitude her religion
She held her breath longer
Longer
And swam further into
The blue.
Waves gently lap
At my feet.
Time leaves.
Distance arrives.

Soon so far out there
A wave's no longer seen
She was the blue
Out there
Out there.

I cupped my hands
To my mouth

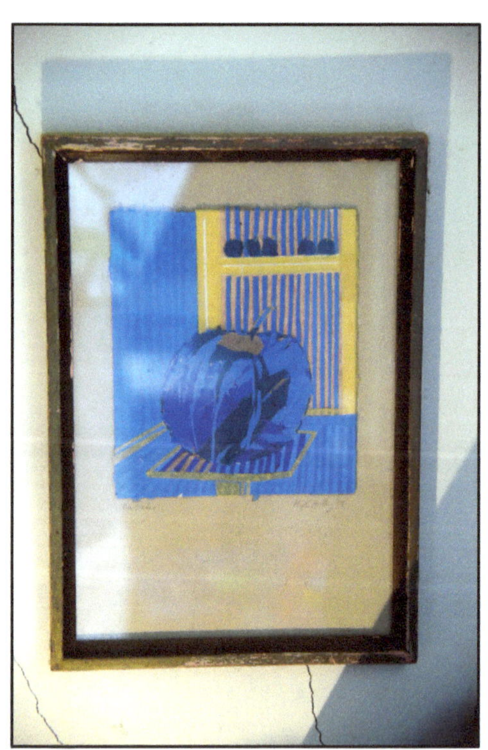

"Change course!
Swim the blue
Parallel to shore!"

My plea fell apart
Out there
Scattered vowels
Floated in the white air.

Brave to swim away.
Braver to stay.

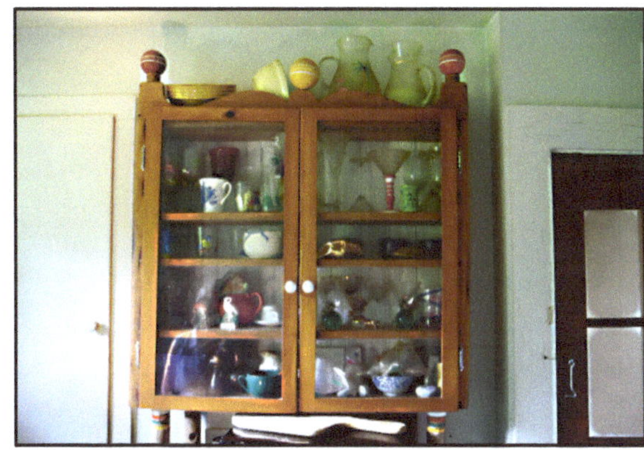

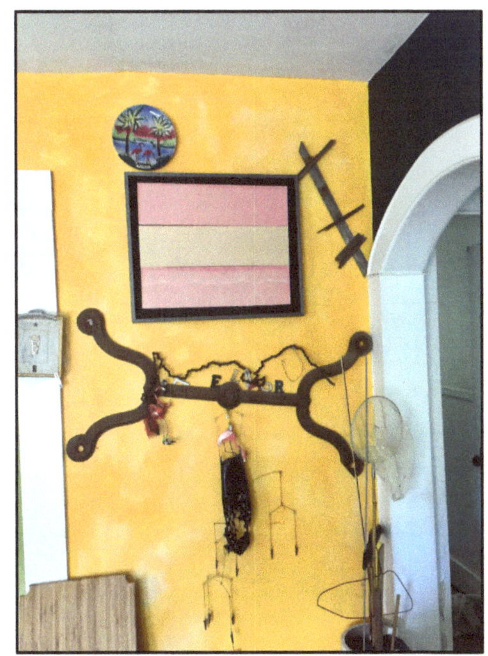

"Large Red Interior –
A calico cat is chased by a dog
Across a carpet of red."

My father holds out his hand
His finger and thumb pinched together.
"What have you got?" I ask.
"A peel." He says.
There is of course
Nothing between finger and thumb.
"But?
A peel of what?"
"A peel," he says "of air."
And laughs
Spitting into the wind
Of illness.
He gets wet.

Once again
My lover jumped over the moon
Ran away with the spoon.
This time
I let go

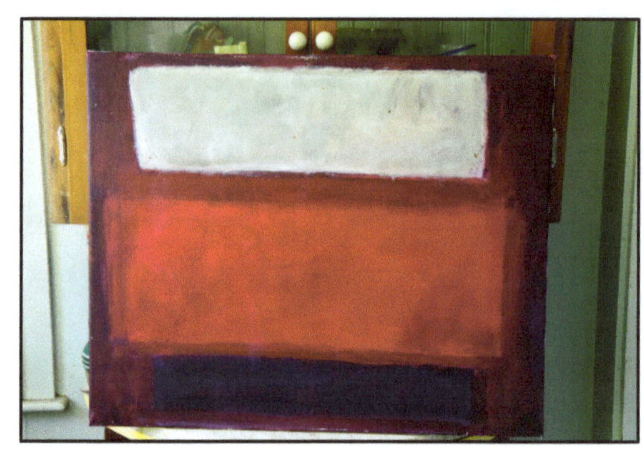

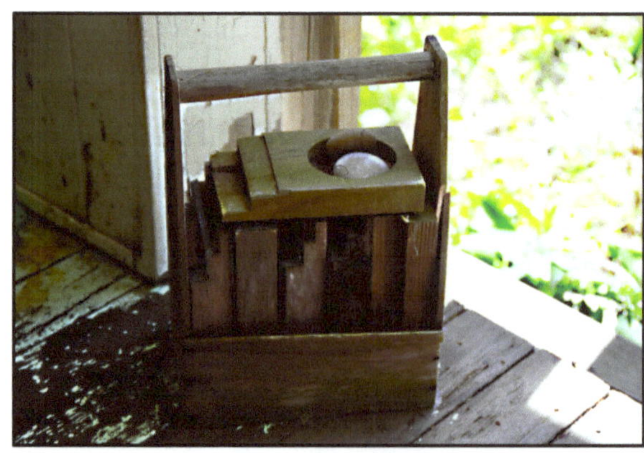

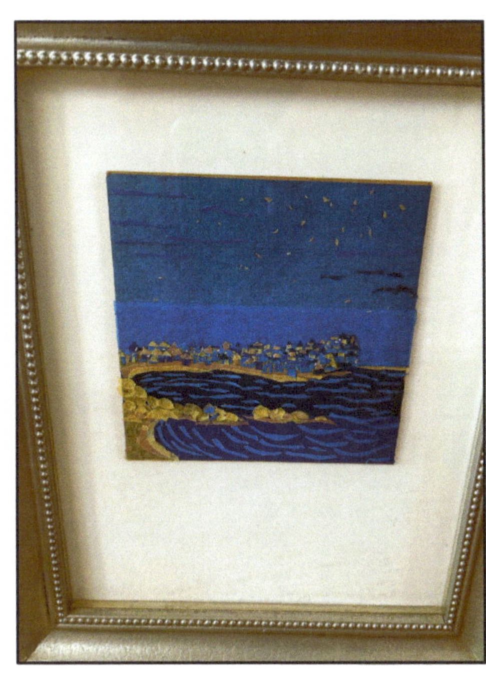

The reminding string
We tied.

"I can carry on."
I said.
When the hurt leaves my head
I will have
Expanded.
Not caught
Small in a box
Or held to the light
Then cast aside
To make way for
Moonleaping flight.

And a dog
Will be chased
Across a carpet of red
By Matisse, the calico cat.
The Carolina wren
Will belt out
Its beautiful tune.
All under
A large blue moon.

I give you
Flower bones
Hard edged
Etched earth tones

Stiff stalked sturdy
More beautiful
Than any pretty petalled
Bloom

More forever
With the rattle
That is
The future.

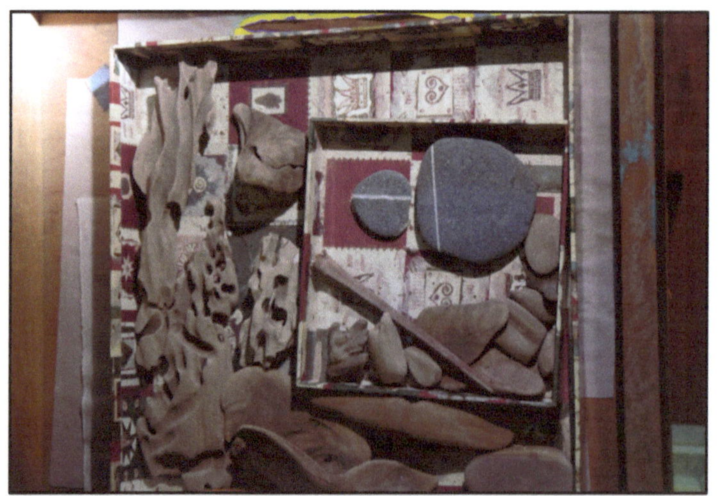

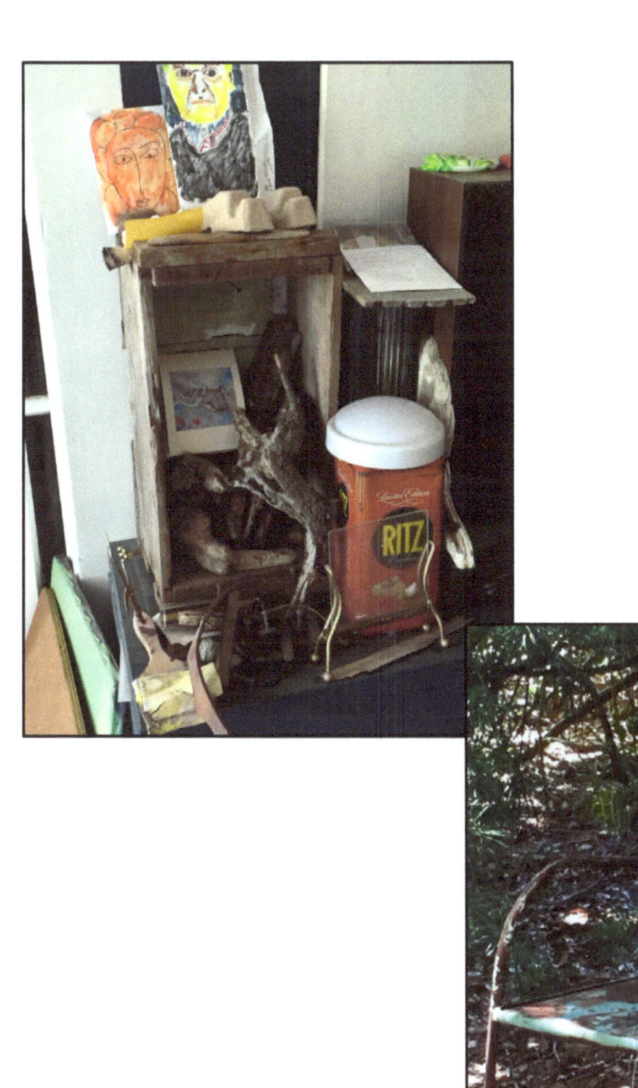

RITZ

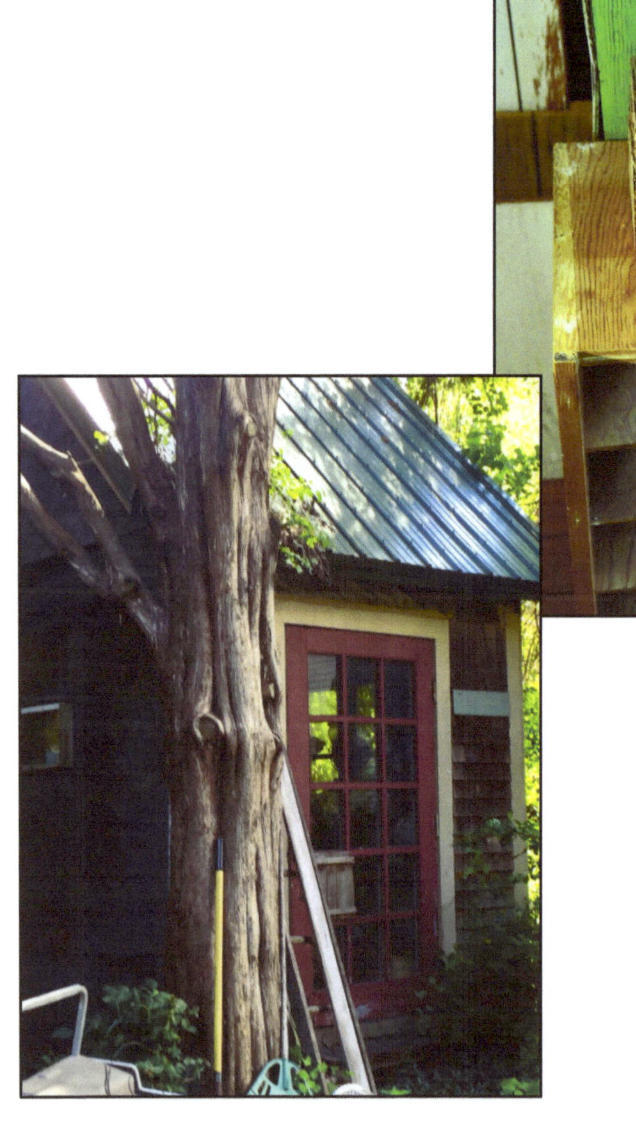

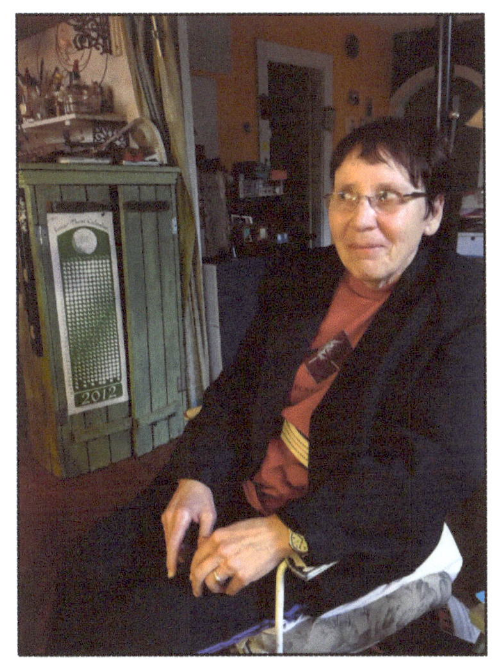

1948-2022